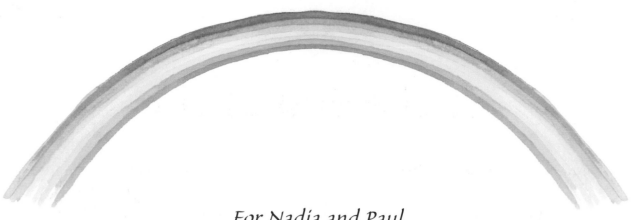

*For Nadia and Paul*
~ A H B

*For Tiziana and Sammy*
~ J B B

LITTLE TIGER PRESS
1 The Coda Centre, 189 Munster Road,
London SW6 6AW, UK
www.littletiger.co.uk

First published in Great Britain 2004
This edition published 2014
by Little Tiger Press, London

Printed in China • LTP/1900/0828/0114

2 4 6 8 10 9 7 5 3 1

This Little Tiger book belongs to:

# At the End of the
# Rainbow

## A. H. Benjamin & John Bendall-Brunello

LITTLE TIGER PRESS

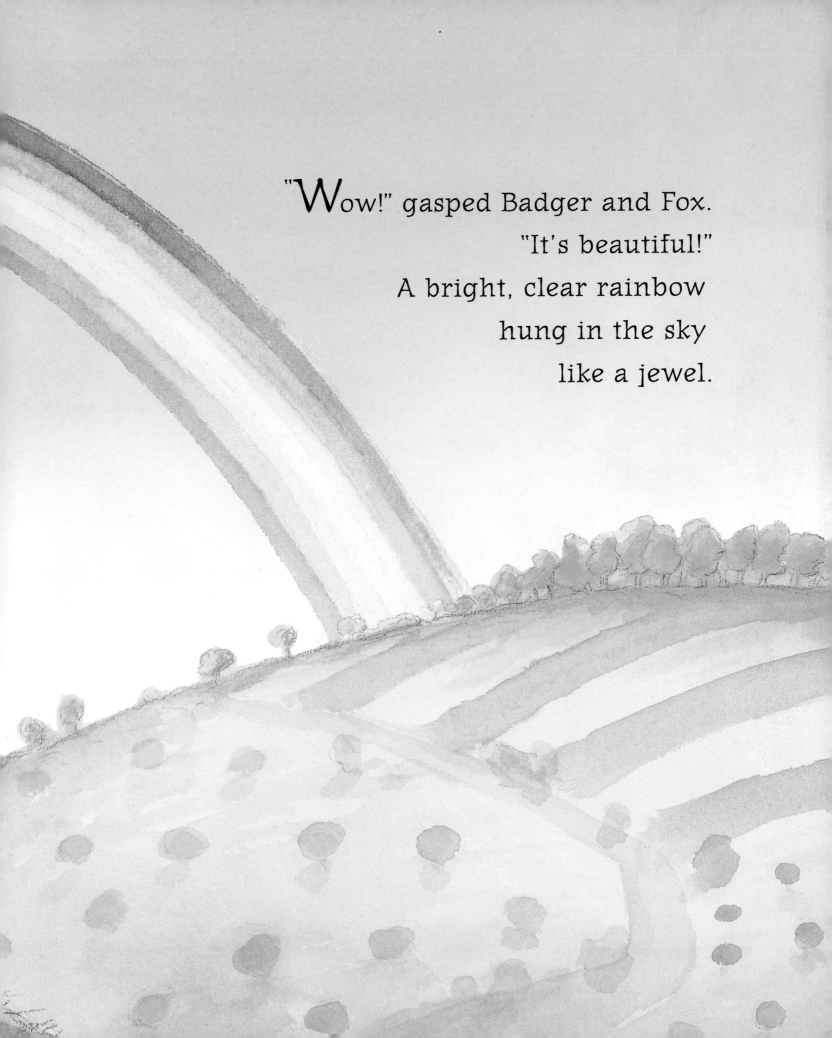

"Wow!" gasped Badger and Fox.
"It's beautiful!"
A bright, clear rainbow
hung in the sky
like a jewel.

Badger and Fox stood gazing at the magnificent rainbow.

Then Badger said, "You know, there's treasure at the end of a rainbow!"

"What's treasure?" asked Fox.

"I'm not sure," replied Badger, "but I think it's gold or silver or jewels—something that will make you rich for ever and ever!"

"I want to go and find this treasure!" cried Fox excitedly.

And they were off, racing into the nearby woods.

As the two friends hurried along
all they could think of was treasure.

What did it look like? Would it be
big or small?

Just then they noticed Squirrel,
sitting in front of a pile of acorns.

"My treasure," he was singing to himself. "My beautiful treasure!"

Badger and Fox scampered up to Squirrel.

"Go away!" he ordered. "You're not stealing my treasure!"

"That's not treasure," said Fox, "that's just a pile of acorns."

"It's treasure to me," replied Squirrel. "It's my food for the winter. What's more important than that?"

"Well, we're going to find the real thing!" said Badger, and the friends raced off.

Soon Badger and Fox came to
a small river. Among the tall grass
they spotted Mother Duck.

"My little treasure!" she was calling.

"Where are you?"

Badger and Fox were curious.

"Are you looking for treasure?" they asked.

"Yes, my own little treasure," replied Mother Duck. "Oh look, there he is!"

A golden, fluffy
duckling came pattering along.
Mother Duck tucked him under her wing.
"Don't disappear like that," she said gently.
"I was worried, my treasure."
Badger and Fox looked puzzled.
"Is that your treasure?" they said.
"Of course," smiled Mother Duck proudly.
"I love my baby more than anything in the
world, so he is a treasure to me. Aren't you,
my little one? Now let's go home."

Badger and Fox rushed on, eager to find their treasure at the end of the rainbow. They clambered up a steep, bumpy hill, and found Old Hare sitting at the top.

"Hello, there!" he greeted.

"Hello!" called the friends. "We're on our way to find treasure!"

"Ahh," nodded Old Hare. "I have lots of that."

"Really? Where?" they asked.

Old Hare patted his head. "Here," he said. "My memories are my treasure. They make me happy."

"What are memories?" asked Badger.

"They're all that you remember from the past," said Old Hare. "Things you've done, places you've visited, friends you've loved. Your adventure today will become a memory you'll treasure, one day. So enjoy yourselves, little ones!"

"Goodbye!" called Badger and Fox. And they were off, sliding down the other side of the hill.

Just then thick, dark clouds filled the sky.
The rainbow vanished. It started to rain,
harder and harder. Badger and Fox had
to take shelter.

"We'll never find our treasure now,"
said Badger miserably.

As they waited for the rain to stop, the friends remembered Squirrel. How happy he was just to have enough food. And Mother Duck and her love for her baby.

Old Hare was happy, too, because he had his memories. They all had their own kind of treasure.

Maybe treasure wasn't gold and silver and jewels. It was what you loved, something very special, and something that made you happy.

Fox looked at Badger, and Badger looked at Fox . . .

"You're a treasure!" said Badger,
jumping up.

"You're a treasure, too," said Fox,
skipping around.

And they started laughing and dancing until they couldn't dance anymore!

At last the rain stopped and the sun came out again. The two friends happily made their way back home. Far, far behind them a new rainbow had appeared in the sky. But neither Badger nor Fox noticed.